# CRUX™

# ATLANTIS RISING

# CRUX

## ATLANTIS RISING

Mark **WAID**
WRITER

Steve **EPTING**
PENCILER

Rick **MAGYAR**
INKER

Frank **D'ARMATA**
COLORIST

### CHAPTER 6

Paul **PELLETIER** · PENCILER

Mark **FARMER** · INKER

Dean **WHITE** · COLORIST

Dave **LANPHEAR** · LETTERER

Steve Epting dedicates this book to his wife Michelle, whose love and support made it possible, and his parents Jim and Betty for their faith and encouragement.

**CrossGeneration Comics    Oldsmar, Florida**

# TABLE OF CONTENTS

# WITHOUT WARNING
## WITHOUT PREPARATION

six survivors of a forgotten race find themselves the galaxy's first,

last, and only line of defense against a merciless alien threat.

Dreamers, artists, and scholars all, they are ill-equipped for battle, but

if they are to survive, they must quickly rise to the challenge now

before them. Victory — or gruesome death — rests upon the speed with

which they can unravel a series of mysteries, beginning with this one:

# WHERE ARE THEY?

The mental and physical abilities of the Atlanteans are identical in nature but not in application.
Capricia and her teammates have each channeled their abilities into different skills:

| CAPRICIA | TUG | ZEPHYRE | GALVAN & GAMMID | VERITYN |
|---|---|---|---|---|
| Shapeshifter and empath | Telekinetic strongman | Hypermetabolic intellectual | Commanders of the electromagnetic spectrum | Seer of all truths |

*Chapter 1 cover art colored by Morry Hollowell*

400,000 B.C.

EARTH

"SO *WHAT* AM I LOOKING FOR, AGAIN?"

"IT ALMOST DOESN'T *MATTER*.

"WHICH, YOU HAVE TO *ADMIT*, IS THE *EXCITING* PART.

"*WHEREVER* YOUR VISION TAKES US, VERITYN, I GUARANTEE WE'LL FIND SOMETHING WORTH THE SEARCH.

"GO ACROSS THE OCEAN AND...OH, I DON'T KNOW, WEST...

"...AND LET'S SEE WHAT WE CAN SEE.

"THERE! THAT FAMILY! WATCH WHAT THAT ALPHA MALE IS DOING!"

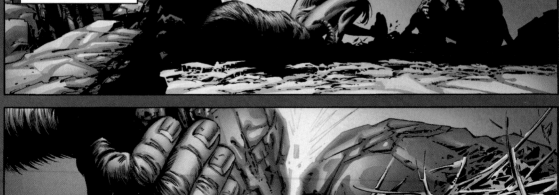

"HE'S BANGING *ROCKS,* CAPRICIA."

"*NO,* DANIK...

"...HE'S *THINKING.*

"THAT'S IT... *THAT'S IT...*

"YES!"

"WAIT! *NO!* IT'S *OKAY!*"

"*TELL* THEM IT'S *OKAY!*"

"*TEACH* THEM."

10,000 B.C.

AM I *DONE?*

YOU'VE BEEN *VERY* HELPFUL, LITTLE SEER.

DON'T *PATRONIZE* ME.

GODS *FORFEND.* THANK YOU FOR SHARING, VERITYN.

*NOW* DO YOU *UNDERSTAND,* DANIK?

I--I THOUGHT OUR ANCESTORS-- *GAVE* THEM FIRE! I--

--SHOULD *REALIZE* THAT OUR FORBEARERS WERE... HOW TO PUT IT?...A LITTLE *FULL* OF THEMSELVES SOMETIMES. *EGO* AND *HISTORY* AREN'T A VERY RELIABLE MIX, DANIK.

MY *POINT* IS *THIS:* JUST BECAUSE OUR ANCESTORS CHOSE TO STEER PRIMITIVE MAN DOWN THEIR--*OUR*-- OWN EVOLUTIONARY PATH--

--THAT DOESN'T GIVE US THE RIGHT TO TAKE CREDIT FOR ALL HUMANITY'S *ACCOMPLISHMENTS.*

THEIR INNATE SENSE OF *DISCOVERY*--THEIR *INDOMITABLE* SPIRIT OF *INVENTION*--THAT WASN'T OUR *GIFT!* THAT WAS *ALWAYS WITHIN* THEM!

THAT'S WHY WE HAVE TO ADMIRE THEM, DANIK--NOT *BELITTLE* THEM!

EVEN *NOW,* THEY'RE CREATING *AGRICULTURAL TECHNOLOGY!* THEY'RE DEVELOPING THEIR OWN *CITIES* AND *MEDICINES* AND *ARCHITECTURE!* WHAT WILL THEY ENVISION *TOMORROW?*

IF WE DO *RIGHT* BY THESE BEINGS... IF WE KEEP OUR ETERNAL *PROMISE* TO WATCH *OVER* THEM...*GUIDE* THEM ONLY WHEN THEY *NEED* IT AND TAKE *PRIDE* IN THEM WHEN THEY *DON'T...*

...THEN SOMEDAY... SOME *AMAZING DAY...* THIS NEW HUMAN RACE WILL NOT ONLY BE OUR *PEERS,* DANIK... THEIR ACHIEVEMENTS WILL MAKE OURS *INSIGNIFICANT* BY *COMPARISON.* SOMEDAY...

AHEM MEANWHILE...

YES?

DEAL'S A DEAL. PAY UP.

I THOUGHT THOSE WHO FOLLOWED THE PATH OF THE SPIRITUAL WERE UNCONCERNED WITH MATERIAL WEALTH.

SO I HEAR. PAY UP.

A POOR CHOICE OF SEERS, CAPRICIA, GIVEN THAT HE ILLUSTRATES MY ARGUMENT.

IS THAT SORT OF PETTY ADHERENCE TO TANGIBLE REWARDS SOMETHING WE TRULY WISH TO FOSTER?

OH, FOR...

HE'S TEN YEARS OLD, DANIK. WE MADE A GAME OF IT.

YOU TRY MOTIVATING A CHILD USING CELESTIAL OVERTURES. BE SURE TO LET ME KNOW HOW IT GOES.

AND HE WAS AN EXCELLENT CHOICE. VERITYN'S A PRODIGY EVEN AMONG THOSE OF HIS PARTICULAR DISCIPLINE.

HE CAN SEE THE TRUTH IN ALL THINGS, DANIK--AND HE'S TAKEN MY SIDE. WHAT DOES THAT TELL YOU?

I DON'T THINK WE'RE ARGUING OVER WHAT THE FUTURE IS, DANIK.

WE'RE DEBATING WHERE IT IS...

THAT, LIKE MOST CHILDREN, HIS WORLD REVOLVES AROUND CANDY TREATS AND CLEVER TOYS.

I, ON THE OTHER HAND, AM AN ADULT. AND I AM FAR MORE CONCERNED WITH OUR FUTURE THAN WITH OUR PRESENT.

...AGAIN. AS WE HAVE MOST OF OUR ADULT LIVES. SO FAMILIAR ARE OUR LINES, THEY'RE PRACTICALLY SCRIPTED. DANIK'S ABOUT TO TELL ME, FOR INSTANCE, THAT THE FUTURE IS WITHIN US.

I DIDN'T MEAN THAT TO SOUND SO ANGRY...

...DID I?

YOU'RE FUMING.

I'M RESPONSIBLE.

AGAIN, AS ARE WE ALL. IN FACT, WHILE YOU TALK AS IF WE'RE FOUNDED IN INDIVIDUALITY, OUR MENTAL AND PHYSICAL ABILITIES ARE IDENTICAL--

--IN NATURE-- BUT NOT IN APPLICATION--

--AND DANIK KNOWS IT. ATLANTEANS EXPRESS THEMSELVES AND HONE THEIR GIFTS BY SPECIALIZING IN ONE OF THE FIVE DISCIPLINES OF ATLANTEAN SOCIETY:

MIND--DOMAIN OF THE TELEPATHS AND TELEKINETICS;

BODY--THOSE ANXIOUS TO REDEFINE THE LIMITATIONS OF FLESH AND BLOOD;

SPIRIT-- DOMINION OF THE SEERS AND PSYCHICS;

PASSION-- CHARACTERISTIC OF THOSE WHO MANIFEST THEIR ENERGIES EXTERNALLY;

AND EMPATHY-- PROVINCE OF THOSE FEW LIKE MYSELF--

--THE SHAPESHIFTERS.

JALEETA? WHAT'S THE MATTER, SWEETIE?

IT'S THE *TRANSITION*, CAPRICIA. WE'VE DECIDED TO STAY BEHIND, BUT JALEETA'S FRIGHTENED.

NOT *JALEETA!* WHY, SHE'S ALWAYS BEEN THE *BRAVEST!*

I WON'T LET *ANYTHING BAD* HAPPEN TO YOU, DARLING. I'LL WATCH OUT FOR *EVERYONE* WHO STAYS, I PROMISE.

THE TRANSITION IS *NOTHING* TO BE *AFRAID* OF.

YOU'RE *STILL* FUMING.

I'M HOPING I DIDN'T *LIE* TO HER. INTELLECTUAL DEBATE *ASIDE*, DANIK... I'M WORRIED ABOUT THE *RAW POWER* THE TRANSITION EVENT STANDS TO UNLEASH.

SUPPOSE YOUR FACTION CAN'T *CONTROL* IT?

THEN YOU'LL STILL BE SAFE IN THE *STASIS CRADLES*. YOU'RE *STILL* FUMING.

I'M *NOT*.

I'M JUST TRYING TO REMEMBER WHEN WE STOPPED BEING *FRIENDS*.

I'VE BEGGED YOU FOR *MONTHS* TO STAY *BEHIND* -- BUT YOU'VE NEVER *ONCE* ASKED *ME* TO COME ALONG WITH *YOUR* GROUP.

I SAW NO *POINT*. I KNEW YOU *WOULDN'T*.

ABSOLUTELY *NOT*. BUT *THAT'S* NOT THE *POINT*.

THE *POINT* IS, YOU *NEVER* ASKED ME.

I HAVE TO *GO*.

ME, *TOO*.

ME, *TOO*.

TWO DAYS LATER, AND WE HAVEN'T SPOKEN SINCE. I WORRY THAT WE NEVER WILL *AGAIN*.

I WONDER IF DANIK FEELS THE *SAME*?

I DOUBT IT.

HE'S AMONG THE *LIKE-MINDED*. AGAINST ALL MY *ADVICE*, HE AND THE VAST MAJORITY OF ATLANTEANS CONGREGATE IN THE *SKY*...

...PREPARING FOR THE CEREMONIAL *POOLING OF POWER* THEY BELIEVE WILL ELEVATE THEM TO AN *ENLIGHTENED STATUS*...

...WHILE THE 1,142 WHO'VE *DECLINED* LOOK TO *ME* TO TELL THEM THAT STAYING *BEHIND* IS A *RATIONAL DECISION*.

ALL MONITORS ARE *ON-LINE* AND *FULLY FUNCTIONAL*?

CHECKED AND DOUBLE-CHECKED.

NO ONE HAS *ANY* REAL IDEA OF WHAT'S ON THE *OTHER SIDE* OF THE *DOOR* ABOUT TO OPEN UP THERE. NEVERTHELESS, WE SHOULD BE SUFFICIENTLY *SHIELDED* AGAINST ANY ENERGY OUTLAY OR BACKLASH.

GOOD. TWO MINUTES *LEFT*, THEN, AND YOU'RE AMONG THE *LAST*. BUT BEFORE WE SECURE YOUR *CRADLE*, MA'AM, ON BEHALF OF US ALL...WELL...

...THANK YOU.

FOR?

FOR REMINDING US WHY WE'RE IN *HERE* INSTEAD OF UP *THERE*. WE'LL CONTINUE TO OVERSEE THE DEVELOPMENT OF THE HUMAN RACE INTO SOMETHING *GRAND*. THAT'S THE *PLAN*, RIGHT?

YES.

THAT'S THE *PLAN*.

THAT'S OUR RESPONSIBILITY.

IT'S TIME.

THREE...TWO... ONE...

SO BRIGHT--! GODS ABOVE, DANIK, WHAT HAVE YOU--

WHAT?

NO!

THE CHAMBER'S COLLAPSING! THE ENTIRE CHAMBER!

WHAT'S HAPPENING? WATER? WHERE'S THE WATER COMING FR--?

WARNING
EMERGENCY SEALS ENGAGED

GOT TO GET OUT! OPEN, DAMN YOU!

WARNING
EMERGENCY SEALS ENGAGED

OPEN!

WARNING
EMERGENCY SEALS ENGAGED

OPENNNNN

*≥KOFF!* *KOFF!*

AIR! I NEED AIR! I--

--I CAN *BREATHE*--? HOW CAN I--*WHY* ARE WE UNDER--?

*AHUH... AHUH...*

OKAY. STAY CALM. FIRST THINGS *FIRST.* BE GRATEFUL THE *QUAKE* HAS STOPPED.

NEXT, MAKE SURE YOU'RE NOT *HURT.* LEGS ARE ALL RIGHT...ARMS...

...*HEAVY?*

*ARMOR?* BUT I WASN'T WEARING *ARMOR...* A *MOMENT* AGO...

A *GIFT.* AS WAS YOUR ABILITY TO DRAW OXYGEN FROM THE SEAWATER.

BOTH SHOULD PROVE *HELPFUL.*

*WHAT? WHY?* WHO ARE *YOU?*

WHAT'S GOING *ON* HERE?

YOU WERE *ASLEEP.* NOW YOU HAVE BEEN *AWAKENED...*

...TO ANSWER A *CALL.*

Huh?

THIS CHAMBER'S A **MAZE** OF MASONRY AND FALLEN CRADLES. EVERY **MOVE** IS AN AMBUSH WAITING TO **HAPPEN**.

VERITYN, OUR GREATEST **SEER**, STANDS THE BEST CHANCE OF **SPOTTING** HIDDEN CREATURES--

*AAAAAAH!*

--PROVIDED WE CAN KEEP HIM **ALIVE**.

I CAN AWAKEN **ONE MORE**. YOUR SELECTION.

BUT LET ME **CAUTION** YOU THAT YOU'RE NOT THINKING LIKE A **WARRIOR**.

THAT *COULD* BE BECAUSE *I'M* **NOT A WARRIOR!** **NONE** OF US ARE!

ONE MORE?

HIM!

BODY, SPIRIT, PASSION, EMPATHY-- **COVERED.**

THAT LEAVES ONLY STUDENTS OF THE **MIND.**

BY AND LARGE, **TELEKINETICS** DO A LOT MORE **SITTING** AND **POINTING** THAN **LIFTING** AND **SWEATING.** YES, THEY **COULD** USE THEIR MENTAL ENERGIES TO **AMPLIFY** THEIR **PHYSICAL STRENGTH...**

..."BUT," THEY FIGURE, "WHY **BOTHER?**"

THERE'S ONLY ONE I **KNOW** OF--

--WHO PREFERS **WORKING WITH HIS HANDS.**

THOOM

Chapter 2 cover art colored by Paul Mounts

I DON'T RECOGNIZE THE BUILDINGS HERE.

I CAN'T READ THE WRITINGS HERE.

I DON'T EVEN KNOW WHERE "HERE" IS...

...EXCEPT THAT IT APPARENTLY HAS SOMETHING TO DO WITH THE RACE OF HUMANS WE PROMISED TO PROTECT...

...BEFORE TAKING A THOUSAND-CENTURY NAP.

THE SMELL OF FRESH SOIL AND THE OCCASIONAL GROUND FLAME TELL ME THE DAMAGE IS FRESH, SO WE'VE BEEN SCOURING THE RUBBLE FOR THE BETTER PART OF AN HOUR.

VERITYN'S UNCOVERED SOME SORT OF SPONGY POINTING DEVICE.

GALVAN AND GAMMID HAVE FOUND A PRIMITIVE WRITING STYLUS...

LET ME SEE THAT.

IN A MINUTE.

...AND SOMETHING NEW TO ARGUE OVER.

HEY! FIND YOUR OWN!

DON'T BE A CHILD.

I SAID "GIVE ME."

ZEPHYRE'S UNEARTHED WHAT WOULD SEEM TO BE A METERED CONVEYANCE. LOTS OF ARTIFACTS...

...BUT NO PEOPLE.

THE *BUGS* DID THIS.

THE *NEGATION?* HAVE YOU *SEEN* THEM? ARE THEY HERE? SHOULD WE--

RELAX. I'M JUST GOING BY *GUT.* I CHOOSE TO BELIEVE THAT NO *CIVILIZED SOCIETY* WOULD CREATE SOMETHING THIS *IMPRESSIVE* JUST TO *WRECK* IT.

WE *ALL* FEEL OUT OF *PLACE,* TUG. BUT SINCE-- FOR RIGHT NOW-- ALL WE HAVE IS *EACH OTHER,* YOU HAVE TO STAY *WITH* US.

WE CAN'T AFFORD FOR YOU TO BUILD WALLS AROUND *YOURSELF.* WE NEED YOU.

FOR *WHAT?* *TK MUSCLE?* WHEN I PICK UP *ATLANTIS,* SHOULD I LIFT WITH MY *LEGS?* WILL THAT *HELP?*

FUNNY. IF I'D WANTED A *COMEDIAN,* BY THE WAY, I'D HAVE PICKED *ZANUSS.*

YOU *SHOULD* HAVE. THE NEGATION WOULD KILL *THEMSELVES* JUST TO AVOID HIS *ACT.*

TELL ME.

*THAT'S RIGHT.* TUG WAS AN *ARCHITECT.* A *BUILDER.* THAT WAS WHERE HE FOUND *BEAUTY.*

*SINCE HE AWOKE,* HE'S BEEN SURROUNDED BY NOTHING BUT *RUINS.*

THIS IS NOT... I DON'T...

I KEEP WANTING TO *WAKE UP,* C. TO THROW OPEN MY *CURTAINS* AND STAND IN THE *SUN* UNTIL IT BURNS AWAY THIS STUPID *NIGHTMARE.*

I REPEAT: *TELL* ME. TUG, IF IT HELPS, WORRY ABOUT *OUR* SITUATION *LATER.* FOR NOW, STAY CENTERED ON WHAT WE HAVE TO MAKE *RIGHT.*

WE WERE *RESPONSIBLE* FOR AN ENTIRE *RACE* THAT'S NOW NOWHERE TO BE *SEEN.*

I DON'T REMEMBER *VOLUNTEERING* TO MAKE THAT *MY PROBLEM* UNDER CIRCUMSTANCES LIKE *THESE.* MY FRIENDS...MY *FAMILY...* THEY'RE ALL...

LOOK, YOU WANT TO TRADE ME OUT FOR SOMEONE WHO SHARES YOUR *PRIORITIES,* TAKE IT UP WITH *RED.*

WHY?

WHY TALK TO *HIM* WHEN I CAN FIND A PERFECTLY GOOD *WALL* TO YELL AT *INSTEAD?*

VERITYN'S SPECIALTY IS TO SEE *TRUTH* IN *ALL* ITS FORMS. LET'S SEE HOW THAT APPLIES TO *CRYPTOLOGY*...

VERITYN, WHAT DOES THIS SAY?

"WE ARE THE *SECURITY ARM* OF *TERRA COGNITO*. COME WITH *US*."

THANK YOU.

DEMONSTRATING NOT ONE MORE *HINT* OF RESISTANCE, WE CALMLY FOLLOW THESE MEN TO THEIR *TRANSPORT VEHICLE*.

SURPRISINGLY, EVEN OUR RED-TRESSED *STRANGER* PUTS UP NO STRUGGLE.

I DON'T LIKE BEING *HERDED*.

DON'T GO *GALVAN* ON ME. I DOUBT THEY'RE ANY *THREAT* TO US, BUT WE SHOULD PLAY *ALONG*...

...UNLESS YOU'VE FIGURED OUT A *BETTER* WAY TO GATHER INFORMATION.

"THOUGHT SO."

AS OUR **MYSTERY MAN** SEEMS TO KNOW, WHILE ALL ATLANTEANS ARE MORE OR LESS CAPABLE OF THE SAME SKILLS, WE EACH REFINE OUR ABILITIES ALONG DIFFERENT **PATHS**...

...THAT "**TERRA COGNITO**," WHATEVER THAT IS, HAS SAFELY EVACUATED THE "**VISITORS**"...WHOEVER **THEY** ARE...

...AND THAT THESE GUARDS (OF **SOMETHING**...) PLAN TO **FOLLOW**, BUT **CAN'T**...

...UNTIL THEY DECIDE WHAT TO DO WITH **US**.

UNFORTUNATELY, THAT'S THE **EXTENT** OF WHAT WE CAN GLEAN. NOTHING'S SAID ABOUT THE HUMAN RACE IN **GENERAL** OR ABOUT THE PLANET'S ODD **TOPOGRAPHY**...

TERRA COGNITO

...SO, DURING *TRANSPORT*, TUG AND VERITYN SILENTLY COMBINE THEIR TALENTS TO COACH THE ENTIRE *GROUP* IN *TELEPATHIC TRANSLATION*.

SLOWLY, WE BEGIN TO FIT THE WORDS OF THE GUARDS TOGETHER LIKE *PUZZLE PIECES* AS WE EAVESDROP.

WE LEARN THAT THE *NEGATION* HAS SWEPT THE GLOBE...

ODD. JUDGING BY THE SIZE OF THIS *FACILITY*, YOU'D THINK THERE'D BE FAR MORE *INHABITANTS*. INSTEAD, WE SEEM TO BE ALL *ALONE*.

...PARTICULARLY SINCE THE GUARDS GROW INCREASINGLY *QUIET*... AND INCREASINGLY *ANXIOUS* FOR SOME REASON.

WHY *IS* THAT?

THE BROTHERS CAN EACH MANIPULATE VARIOUS **RADIATIONS**.

**GALVAN'S** FAVORITE IS **INFRARED**, **GAMMID'S** IS **ULTRAVIOLET**.

BOTH PROVE **EFFECTIVE DESPITE** THE TWINS HAVING **NO CLUE** HOW BEST TO USE THEM IN COMBAT.

WE'RE **OVERWHELMED**... FORCED INTO BATTLE NOT OUT OF **COURAGE** SO MUCH AS SOME MIXTURE OF **ADRENALINE** AND **BLIND PANIC**.

**OURS** WAS --

-- IS A RACE FOUNDED ON **PEACE** AND **TRANQUILITY**. WE'RE NOT USED TO PUTTING OURSELVES AT **RISK**...

...NOR AM I CONFIDENT WE'D AGREE ON WHAT'S WORTH RISKING OUR LIVES TO **PROTECT**.

KE7? KREE!

?

KE7? KREE!

WE ALL HAVE OUR PRIORITIES.

I RAN *AHEAD* TO FIND A *CLEAN CORRIDOR* OUT! LET'S *GO!*

THEY'RE RIGHT *BEHIND* US! *HURRY!*

GOT

HIM!

THE GUARDS *GET* IT. BETWEEN ZEPH'S *TONE* AND HER FRANTIC *GESTURES*, THERE'S NOT MUCH ROOM FOR *MISINTERPRETATION*.

THEY STORM DOWN THE HALLS IN TENSE *SILENCE*. ONLY ONCE, AS WE NEAR THE CORRIDOR'S *END*, DO THEY *SPEAK*--AND WHILE I STRAIN TO *UNDERSTAND* THEM --

OH GOD! LET! ᑫᒷ ᒷᒷᒷ ᒷᒷᒷ ᒷᒷᒷᒷᒷ!

ᑫᒷᒷ ᒷᒷᒷᒷᒷ GO ᒷᒷᒷᒷᒷ?

ᒷᒷᒷ GO ᒷᒷᒷᒷᒷᒷ ᒷᒷᒷᒷ!

--IT BECOMES HARD TO CONCENTRATE.

A FEW MINUTES LATER, THE **FINAL TRANSPORT** BEGINS ITS VOYAGE TO THE **STARS**.

I WONDER IF WE SHOULD BE **ABOARD**...

CRUX CHAPTER 3

...THIS IS WHAT HAPPENED TO OURS.

STILL, I THINK WE CAN MAKE IT *RIGHT*... AND I MUST BE ON TO SOMETHING IF THE *STRANGER'S* DEIGNED TO *JOIN* US IN OUR WORK.

THEN AGAIN, HE COULD JUST STOP AT ANY MOMENT AND CONTEMPLATE HIS NAVEL. HE'S LIKE THAT.

I FIND HIM *MORE* THAN A LITTLE *MADDENING*. YES, HE WOKE THE SIX OF US UP TO FIGHT THE *NEGATION*...

IF *ANYBODY* ON THE TEAM HAS FIGURED HIM OUT...

...I'D *LOVE* TO KNOW *WHAT* THEY *SEE*.

...BUT HE STILL WON'T SAY *WHY*, OR WHO *HE* IS, OR PASS ALONG MUCH OF *ANYTHING* THAT MIGHT RESEMBLE, OH, *INFORMATION*.

NEVER MIND. CONCENTRATE ON THE TASK AT *HAND*.

BEFORE WE LEFT *TERRA COGNITO*, *ZEPHYRE*--LEARNING EARTH LANGUAGES ALONG THE *WAY*--RESEARCHED IN *ONE AFTERNOON* THOUSANDS OF *YEARS'* WORTH OF ANTI-GRAVITY RESEARCH AND DEVELOPMENT...

...*LOVING* EVERY MINUTE OF IT, PROFESSIONAL *STUDENT* THAT SHE *IS*.

NO WONDER SHE'D RATHER SPEND TIME WITH HER *STUDIES* THAN WITH HER *PEERS*:

LISTEN LISTEN *LISTEN* THIS IS JUST *REMARKABLE* WHAT THEY'VE DISCOVERED ABOUT THE RELATIONSHIP BETWEEN GRAVITY AND *ELECTROMAGNETISM* AND HOW WHAT THEY CALL *BOSONS* AND *FERMIONS* ARE TIED TOGETHER IN A *UNIFIED THEORY* THEY CALL *SUPERSTRING* WHICH MEANS THAT *ENERGY* HAS SOME PROPERTIES OF *MATTER* AND MATTER HAS SOME PROPERTIES OF *ENERGY* AND *AND* WE CAN *WORK* WITH THAT TO

BOOKS AND COMPUTERS CAN KEEP *UP* WITH HER...

CONFIGURE A SERIES OF TOWE— TO PROVIDE A FERMION WAVE—

Uh-huh. TUG, *YOU* UNDERSTAND HER, RIGHT?

YEP. THEN WE'RE GOOD.

I LOVE ZEPH, BUT GET HER WORKED *UP* AND SHE'S LIKE A KID TELLING A JOKE: "AND THEN—AND *THEN*—AND *THEN*—"

AND THOUGH WE NOW HAD A *PLAN*, EVEN WITH ZEPH'S NEW-FOUND KNOWLEDGE AND SOME SPARE *COGNITO* TECHNOLOGY—

—WE REQUIRED *SOME* EQUIPMENT STILL TOO ADVANCED FOR *EARTH*—

OVER *HERE*.

—BUT NOT FOR *ATLANTIS*.

WHICH IS WHY I'VE TEAMED VERITYN, OUR *SEER*, WITH TUG, THE FORMER ARCHITECT AND *BUILDER*...

CHECK.

...TO FIND ANY AND EVERY PIECE OF SALVAGEABLE ATLANTEAN TECHNOLOGY REGARDLESS OF HOW DEEPLY IT'S *BURIED*.

NOT THAT THERE'S MUCH LEFT AFTER 100,000 YEARS *UNDERSEA*...

NO, NO, NO. DOWN *THERE*. YOU GOTTA *REACH*.

SURE. HOLD *THIS*.

HAR.

...BUT FOLLOWING TUG'S *INSTRUCTIONS*, GALVAN AND *GAMMID* MELD THE *SCRAPS* TO THE *COGNITO* PARAPHERNALIA, RINGING ATLANTIS WITH A SERIES OF *TOWERS*...

...THAT, ONCE *COMPLETED*, SHOULD RAISE ATLANTIS TO THE *SURFACE* ONCE MORE.

IN THE MEANTIME, THE TWINS HAVE COMBINED THEIR *POWER* TO GIVE US A "SUN" THAT PROVIDES *WORKLIGHT*.

LET'S HOPE THEY CAN *MAINTAIN* THAT SPIRIT OF COOPERATION. INDIVIDUALLY, THEY'RE BOTH QUITE *GIFTED*—

—BUT THEIR *UNITED* POWER SETS *NEW* LEVELS—

—WHEN AND *ONLY* WHEN THEY'RE ACTING TOGETHER, IN HARMONY, IN SYNCH, IN *RHYTHM*. AND THEREIN...

--IS THAT THE ALIENS ARE LIKE **BUGS**. THEY SHOW NO SIGN OF BEING AN ACTUAL ORGANIZED **ARMY** WITH STRATEGY AND PLANNING AND **WEAPONS**. OTHERWISE--

--WE WOULDN'T STAND A **CHANCE**.

SO WHAT'S GNAWING AT THE TWINS, VERITYN? BETTER YET, WHY IN THE NAME OF THE *LIFEGODS* WOULD IT EVEN STILL BE AN *ISSUE* GIVEN ALL THAT'S HAPPENED *SINCE?*

PEOPLE ARE *FUNNY.*

THANKS. HOW ABOUT *YOU? YOU'RE* SO SMART. DO *YOU* HAVE ANY INSIGHTS YOU'D LIKE TO SHARE?

HERE. LET ME *ANSWER* FOR YOU. "NO."

WHEW! *BREAK!*

LET ME TELL YOU, THE DOWNSIDE TO *ACCELERATING* YOUR *METABOLISM...*

...IS THE ABILITY TO WORK UP A *SWEAT* EVEN AT THE BOTTOM OF THE *OCEAN.*

I CAN'T *IMAGINE.* ZEPH, YOU KNEW THE TWINS FROM...BEFORE. AM I *FORGETTING?* WERE THEY *ALWAYS* THIS *BAD?*

NOT REALLY, NO.

THEN WHAT IS IT THAT'S COME *BETWEEN* THEM?

MAYBE SOME STUPID *PRIDE* THING? MAYBE A *WOMAN.* WHO KNOWS?

BACK TO WORK.

HUH. SOME SORT OF *ROMANTIC* ENTANGLEMENT, SHE SAYS...

...WHICH, BY THE WAY, WAS AN UNCHARACTERISTICALLY *INTROSPECTIVE* THEORY FOR ZEPH TO OFFER *UP...*

...ALMOST AS IF...

AND SO CONCLUDES A *LOVELY LITTLE INTERLUDE,* THEN. HERE'S A LESSON I DIDN'T WANT TO LEARN:

THE *NEGATION* IS SMARTER THAN WE *THOUGHT.*

VERITYN, WE'RE ALMOST FINISHED WITH THE *TOWERS.* WILL YOU KEEP *WATCH...*

...AND NEXT TIME, MENTION THE WORD "*AX*" A LITTLE *SOONER?*

'KAY.

SHE PUTS A GREAT DEAL OF *TRUST* IN YOU. IT SEEMS YOU HAVE QUITE THE *GIFT.*

NAH. MORE LIKE AN *APTITUDE.* *ALL* THE ATLANTEANS ARE PRETTY MUCH THE SAME THAT WAY. WE JUST TEND TO *SPECIALIZE.*

BUT YOU *KNOW* THAT.

HOW *WOULD* I?

Oh, COME *ON.* I'VE BEEN A *SEER* EVER SINCE I WAS A *LITTLE KID.*

AS OPPOSED TO --?

I C'N LOOK AT STUFF AND SEE *TRUTH.* WHAT'S *REALLY THERE.* YOU KNOW *THAT,* TOO.

I KNOW YOU ENJOY *BARTERING* FOR WHAT KNOWLEDGE YOU *GLEAN.*

THE SHORT EXPLANATION IS **THIS:**

**GRAVITY IS OVERRATED.**

IT TAKES THE GRAVITATIONAL FORCE OF OUR **ENTIRE PLANET** TO HOLD A SHARD OF METAL **DOWN**--

--BUT EVEN THE **TINIEST MAGNET** CAN PICK IT **UP.**

**ELECTROMAGNETIC FORCE** IS THE **TRUE POWERHOUSE.** BECAUSE **MATTER**-- A.K.A. **FERMIONS**--AND **ENERGY**-- A.K.A. **BOSONS**-- ARE THE TWO **HALVES** OF ELECTROMAGNETISM--

--THEY AFFECT ONE ANOTHER SO **DIRECTLY** AND **DRAMATICALLY** THAT THE BEST **GRAVITY** CAN DO IS WATCH FROM THE **SIDELINES.**

**ATLANTIS,** LIKE **ALL** SOLID MATTER, IS ESSENTIALLY A COLLECTION OF **FERMIONS.**

AND SINCE THE TWINS **GALVAN** AND **GAMMID** ARE, FOR ALL INTENTS AND PURPOSES, **LIVING BOSONS**--

--**THEY** CAN WRENCH ATLANTIS **FREE** FROM THE CONSTRAINTS OF **EARTHLY GRAVITY.**

"...ACCOMPLISHING *SOMETHING!*"

ARE THE *MECHANICS* FLAWED?

*VERITYN'S* A *SEER*, RIGHT? CAN HE TAKE A LOOK *INSIDE?*

IF HE WERE *NEARBY.*

HE'S NOT IN YOUR *CARE?* THE *NEGATION--*

-- DOESN'T NEED TO ADD A *TEN-YEAR-OLD* TO THEIR LIST OF *VICTIMS.*

THAT'S WHY I SENT HIM *AWAY* WITH THE *STRANGER...*

"...TO KEEP HIM OUT OF *TROUBLE.*"

SOME SORT OF *FANCIFUL TOY?*

YAWN.

AN *UNLIMITED* SUPPLY OF *CANDY?*

WHAT AM I, A *CHILD?*

YOU DON'T HAVE MANY *FRIENDS* YOUR AGE, DO YOU?

*NO!* WHAT'S *THAT* ABOUT?

I'M *LEARNING.*

SO HOW LONG HAVE YOU KNOWN THAT I'M *DANIK?*

WHAT DO *YOU* THINK? SINCE I LAID *EYES* ON YOU.

AND YET, YOU SAID *NOTHING* TO THE *OTHERS...*

...YET...

...YET...

...'CAUSE *CAPRICIA* HATES YOU...

...WHICH IS PROBABLY WHY YOU CHANGED YOUR *FACE,* RIGHT? IF SHE'D *RECOGNIZED* YOU, SHE'D LOP YOUR *HEAD* OFF...

...SO I'VE KEPT MY *MOUTH* SHUT...FOR *NOW...*'CAUSE I BET THAT *LOPPABLE HEAD* CAN FIGURE OUT A BETTER *BRIBE* FOR MY *SILENCE* THAN *CANDY.*

*SEERS* DON'T TRADITIONALLY HAVE SUCH A *MERCENARY ATTITUDE* TOWARDS THEIR *GIFT* OF *TRUE SIGHT.*

BLAH, BLAH. LESS TALKING, MORE *BRIBING.*

WHAT?

-- SHE'D BE DEAD.

WE ARE.

CAPRICIA!

I DON'T NEED TO HEAR ZEPHYRE SCREAMING. HER CRY COMES TELEPATHICALLY--

--AND WE'LL BE AT HER SIDE BEFORE THE SOUND OF HER VOICE COULD HAVE REACHED US.

JUST FROM HER TONE, I CAN TELL THIS ATTACK MAKES THE LAST ONE LOOK LIKE A PRACTICE RUN. I DID THE RIGHT THING IN DISMISSING VERITYN.

"--WE DON'T *HAVE* TO USE NULL-GRAV ON AN ENTIRE *ISLAND CITY*--"

"--JUST ON THE VERMIN CRAWLING *THROUGH* IT!"

THEY'RE *GONE!*

THEN *DON'T STOP!* GIVE IT *EVERYTHING!* WE CAN *DO THIS!*

OUR *FRIENDS--* OUR *FAMILIES--* THEY'RE *COUNTING ON US!*

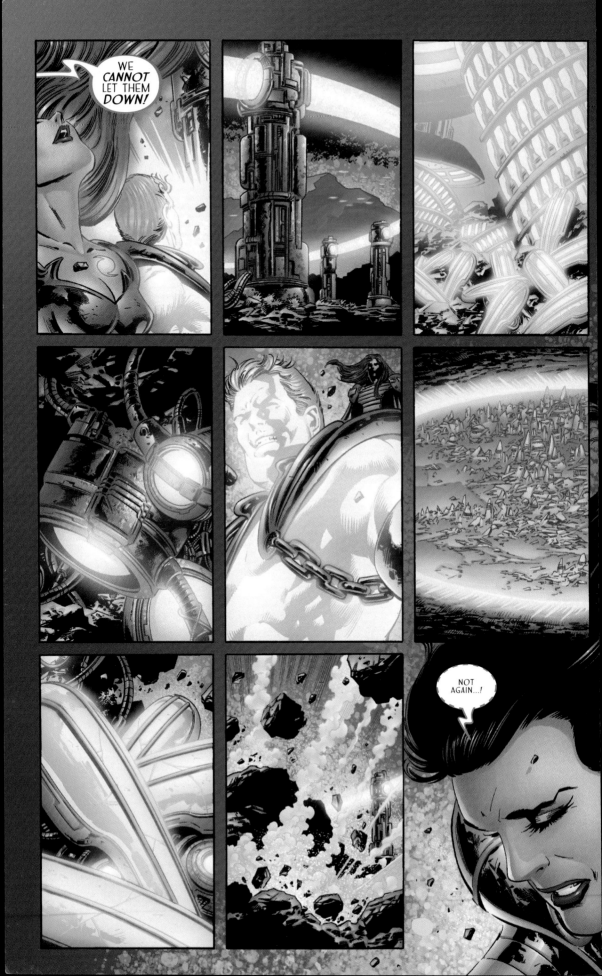

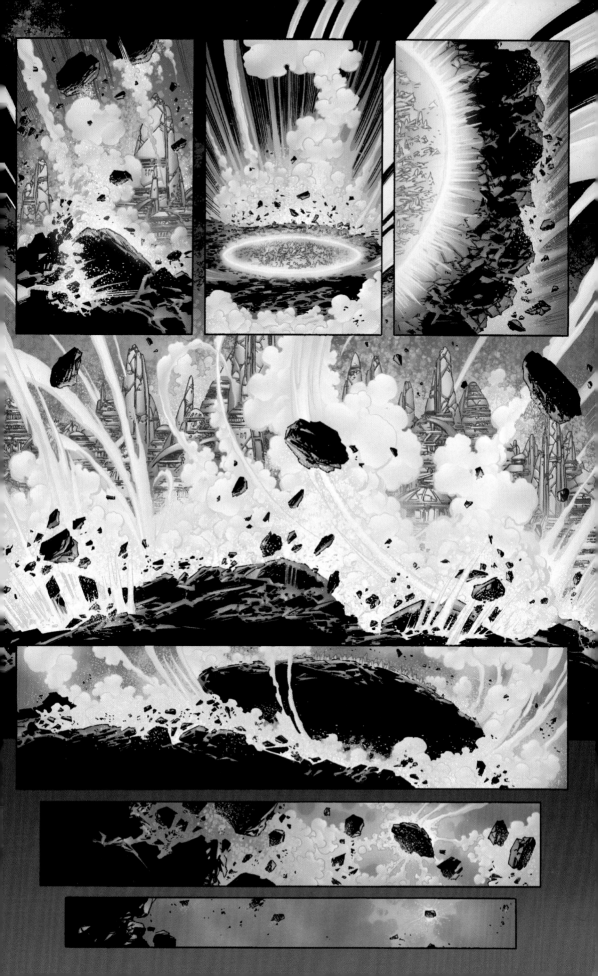

EVERYTHING'S BLACK.

I DON'T EVEN REALIZE MY EYES ARE CLOSED UNTIL I'M OVERCOME BY A FAMILIAR SMELL.

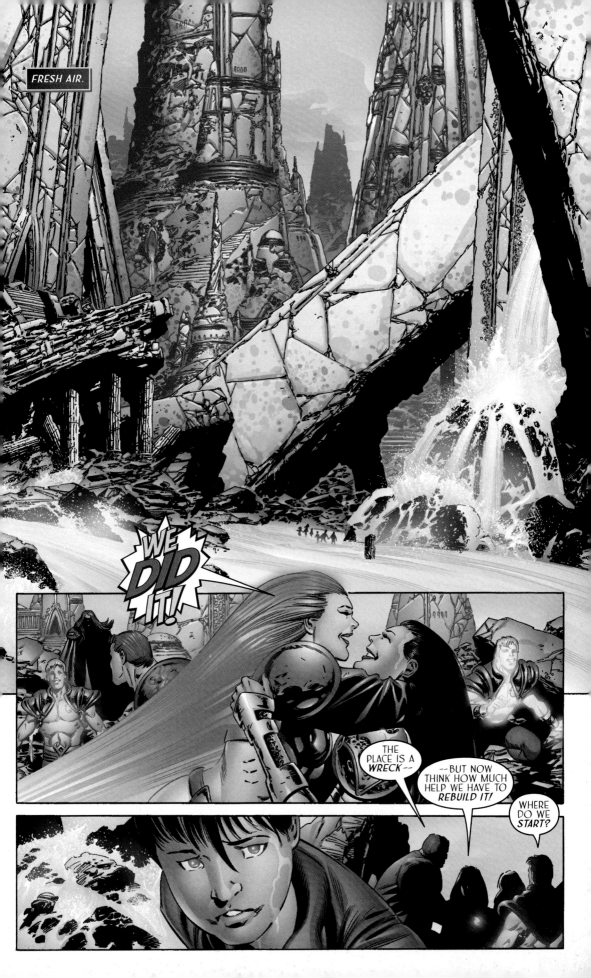

CRUX CHAPTER 5

VERITYN, WAKE *UP.* TODAY'S THE *BIG DAY.*

YOU MEAN WE'RE GOING WITH *DAD?*

YOUR FATHER ISN'T *JOINING* US...

...RIGHT... *NOW,* I MEAN.

Oh.

WE HAVE TO GET TO THE *STASIS CHAMBERS* BEFORE *TRANSITION.* YOU'LL BE *SAFE* THERE.

BUT *DAD--*

VERITYN, *PLEASE!* THIS IS *NOT* A DEBATE, AND WE HAVE *NO* TIME TO *WASTE!* GET DRESSED...

...SO I CAN CONTINUE USING YOU AS AN *EXCUSE*...AND PRAY THE GODS CAN *FORGIVE* ME FOR SUCH A VILE ACT.

I'M *NOT* FEARFUL FOR MY SON. I'M AFRAID OF ABANDONING A WORLD IN WHICH I FEEL *NEEDED.* WHERE MY ACHIEVEMENTS *MEAN* SOMETHING.

WHERE THEY *DEFINE* ME.

I'M AFRAID FOR *ME*...AND THAT IS WHAT *DAMNS* ME. IN GARWIN'S EYES, I AM LOVED BECAUSE I AM *STRONG.* TO ADMIT *FEAR*...

I CAN ONLY *IMAGINE* HIS *REVULSION.* I COULD NEVER *BEAR* HIS *DISGUST.*

I LOVE HIM TOO MUCH.

CAPRICIA, HOW FORTUNATE ARE WE TO FINALLY HAVE REACHED THE POINT OF *ULTIMATE EVOLUTION?*

A TRANSITION THAT WILL TAKE US TO THE NEXT LEVEL OF *EXISTENCE?*

WHY IS YOUR *MINORITY FACTION* SO *OPPOSED* TO FULFILLING ITS *DESTINY?*

WE'RE A PATIENT GROUP, DANIK. WE'LL *GLADLY* BRAVE *ANY* TRANSITION ONCE THE HUMAN RACE CAN DO *WITHOUT* US. IN THE *MEANTIME...*

NOT *JALEETA!* WHY, SHE'S ALWAYS BEEN THE *BRAVEST!*

I WON'T LET *ANYTHING BAD* HAPPEN TO YOU, DARLING. I'LL WATCH OUT FOR *EVERYONE* WHO STAYS BEHIND. I *PROMISE.*

CRUX CHAPTER 6

*Chapter 6 cover art penciled by Paul Pelletier, inked by Rick Magyar, and colored by Frank D'Armata*

WE WERE IN MOS... ...MOSCHO? MOSSTO? *SOMETHING* LIKE THAT...

...BUT, LIKE EVERYTHING ELSE ON EARTH, NOT *QUITE* "THAT." SOME TIME AFTER HUMANITY'S *DISAPPEARANCE,* THE *TERRA COGNITO* CORPORATION REMADE EARTH INTO AN *AMUSEMENT PARK-SLASH-MUSEUM*...

...RECREATING DIFFERENT ERAS OF TERRAN HISTORY SIDE BY *SIDE.* JUST *TODAY,* WE'D WALKED THROUGH *"FIFTH CENTURY JAPAN"* AND *"NEPAL, 5040 A.D."* WHATEVER *"A.D."* SIGNIFIES....

...TO GET *HERE* IN SEARCH OF *CLUES.* GEROMI, OUR TERRA COGNITO *"TOUR GUIDE"* AND SELF-PROFESSED *"HISTORY GEEK"*...AGAIN, WHATEVER *THAT* MEANS... SAYS MOSCOW...

(THAT'S IT. MOSCOW.)

...*MOSCOW* IS RUMORED TO HOLD SOME *SIGNIFICANCE* IN THE LEGENDS OF HUMANITY'S SUDDEN *DISAPPEARANCE.* GEROMI'S VERY *HELPFUL* THAT WAY...

...WHEN HE'S GOT HIS MIND ON HIS *WORK.*

--REALLY LIKE YOUR *HAIR* TODAY, ZEPH. YRE. ZEPHYRE. I MEAN, CAN I CALL YOU *"ZEPH"*? 'CAUSE, LIKE, IF THAT'S NOT *OKAY,* I'LL--

IT'S *FINE,* GEROMI.

COOL. ZEPH. COOL. HEY, YOU CAN CALL ME *"GER"* IF YOU LIKE.

NO, WAIT. THAT'S STUPID. I MEAN ⇒KZZK KZZZTTKKK⇐

Huh. HE SOUNDS POSITIVELY *BROKEN UP* OVER YOU.

AAAAAAAAA!

DAMN YOU, ARE YOU PROUD? YOU WERE RIGHT ABOUT PUSHING VERITYN TOO FAR! I ADMIT IT! ARE YOU HAPPY NOW?

WILL YOU ADMIT AT LEAST THAT MUCH?

WILL YOU EVER SAY ANYTHING AT ALL?!

...WE OUGHT TO KEEP *MOVING.* NO TELLING WHEN THOSE *NEGATION* CREEPS'LL POP BACK UP.

ANYBODY KNOW WHAT COMES *NEXT?*

NOT "CAPRICIA." "ANYBODY." SAID NOT BY *ACCIDENT.*

AFTER WHAT I LET HAPPEN --

-- NO -- WHAT I *DID* TO VERITYN -- ANY *RESPECT* THE OTHERS HAD FOR ME IS *GONE.*

MY LOAD IS *LIGHTER,* TRUE. AND ALL I HAD TO *TRADE* FOR IT...WAS THEIR *TRUST.*

WITHOUT IT, WE HAVE *NOTHING* TO HOLD US *TOGETHER.* I HAVE TO FIND A WAY TO EARN IT *BACK.*

AND *GEROMI'S* GOING TO *HELP* ME...

# CAPRICIA
## SHAPESHIFTER AND EMPATH

*Pin-up art drawn and inked by Steve Epting
with colors by Frank D'Armata.*

# CAPRICIA
## SHAPESHIFTER AND EMPATH

*Pin-up art drawn and inked by Steve Epting
with colors by Frank D'Armata.*

# CROSSGEN COMICS

## Graphic Novels

**THE FIRST 1**
Two Houses Divided $19.95 1-931484-04-X

**THE FIRST 2**
Magnificent Tension $19.95 1-931484-17-1


**MYSTIC 1**
Rite of Passage $19.95 1-931484-00-7

**MYSTIC 2**
The Demon Queen $19.95 1-931484-06-6


**MERIDIAN 1**
Flying Solo $19.95 1-931484-03-1

**MERIDIAN 2**
Going to Ground $19.95 1-931484-09-0


**SCION 1**
Conflict of Conscience $19.95 1-931484-02-3

**SCION 2**
Blood for Blood $19.95 1-931484-08-2


**SIGIL 1**
Mark of Power $19.95 1-931484-01-5

**SIGIL 2**
The Marked Man $19.95 1-931484-07-4


**CRUX 1**
Atlantis Rising $15.95 1-931484-14-7


**SOJOURN 1**
From the Ashes $19.95 1-931484-15-5


**CROSSGEN ILLUSTRATED**
Volume 1 $24.95 1-931484-05-8